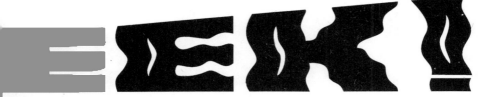

EEK!
Stories to make you shriek™

**For Beginning Readers
Ages 6-8**

This series of spooky stories has been created especially for beginning readers—children in first and second grades who are developing their reading skills.

How do these books help children learn to read?
- Kids love creepy stories and these stories are true page-turners (but never too scary).
- The sentences are short.
- The words are simple and repeated often in the story.
- The type is large with lots of room between words and lines.
- Full-color pictures on every page act as visual "clues" to help children figure out the words on the page.

Once children have read one story, they'll be asking for more!

Library of Congress Cataloging-in-Publication Data

Herman, Gail, 1959–
    The haunted bike / by Gail Herman ; illustrated by Blanche Sims.
        p.   cm. — (Eek! Stories to make you shriek)
    Summary: When Emma acquires a haunted bike with strange powers, it takes her to the home of an oddly dressed boy who once had a similar bike.
    [1. Bicycles and bicycling—Fiction. 2. Ghosts—Fiction.] I. Sims, Blanche, ill.
II. Title. III. Series.
PZ7.H4315Has   1996
[Fic]—dc20   95-18329
                                                                                    CIP
ISBN 0-448-41269-1   A B C D E F G H I J   AC

EEK!

stories to make you shriek™

The Haunted Bike

By Gail Herman
Illustrated by Blanche Sims

Grosset & Dunlap • New York

There is no such thing as a haunted bike.

Everyone knows that.

But I'll tell you a story,

a story I have never told before.

It's about something that happened

a long, long time ago.

I was just a little girl.

Listen to my story.

Then see what you believe.

It all started one afternoon.

My family had moved to a new town.

I was sitting on the front steps

of our house.

I was lonely and bored.

I watched the big kids on their bikes.

A boy named Jake sped by me.

His bike was shiny and new.

"Hey, Emma," he called.

"Want to try my bike?"

I wanted to ride a bike
more than anything.
But I was surprised.
Jake was never nice.
He was a big bully.

"You mean it?" I asked.

Jake stopped.

He smiled as he came close.

"Of course," he said.

"Of course NOT!"

Jake laughed and rode away.

Some of the other kids laughed, too.

I went inside and slammed the door.

Soon my father came home.

"My little pumpkin," he said,

"I have a surprise for you."

And guess what?

It was a bike!

My family was poor,

so it was not a new bike.

The paint was chipped.

And the handles were rusty.

But to me it was the best

bike in the world.

"Papa! Thank you!"

I ran and hugged him.

I wanted to try out my bike right away.

I didn't know how to ride, of course.

And I expected that it would be hard.

But I got on the bike.

And what do you know?

Off I went!

Slowly at first.

Then faster and faster.

How strange!

It was as if I had nothing to do with it.

The bike seemed to go all by itself.

Papa waved as I whizzed by.

He looked surprised and proud.

I tried to wave back.

"Oh, Emma, watch out!" he warned.

Too late, I saw the tree.

I did not know how to steer.

I thought I was a goner.

But somehow the bike swerved.

It seemed to do it all on its own.

And I missed the tree.

I was shaken up.

But the next day

I wanted to try my bike again.

Mama said, "You may go on a longer ride.

But do not go too far."

So I got on my bike.

Just like before,

it was as easy as pie.

I remember thinking,

it's like the bike is riding itself.

I did not know how right I was!

I rode down one block,

then another.

At one corner I tried

to make a left turn.

But the bike went right.

How strange!

At the next corner I tried to go right.

But this time the bike went left.

This was <u>very</u> strange.

The bike seemed to know

where it wanted to go.

But that was silly,

I told myself.

There must be something wrong

with the steering.

I was pretty far from home now.

The houses were far apart.

They were big and fancy.

But the streets were empty,

except for a boy.

He stood in front of a big white house.

The boy smiled and waved
as if he had been waiting for me.
His clothes were old-fashioned.
But he seemed nice.
So I waved back.

24

SCREECH!

The bike stopped by itself

right in front of his house!

I swear it was not me!

25

"I used to have a bike like that,"

the boy said.

"I could do all kinds of tricks on it.

If you want, I can show you some."

"Sure," I said.

And I let him have a ride.

The boy was good!

He could ride without hands.

He could make a sharp turn
with one foot on the ground.

Then he asked if

I wanted to learn some tricks.

Did I?

Of course.

And I was good at them, too!

Once again it crossed my mind.

This can't be just me.

The bike is helping me.

Soon it was time to go.

Mama would start to worry.

"Want to come to my house tomorrow?"
I asked the boy.

All at once, he backed away.

"No," he said softly,

"I can't."

He started to go.

"Wait!" I cried.

"What's your name?"

"Bobby," said the boy.

"Come back tomorrow.

I'll show you more tricks."

His voice trailed off.

And he disappeared into the house.

The next day I rode back to the house,

and the day after that,

and the day after that.

It was always easy finding it.

The bike seemed to know the way.

And each time, Bobby was waiting.

I was so happy to have a friend!

Bobby showed me how to lift

my front tire up in the air,

and how to spin around and around.

But Bobby never asked me inside his house.

And he would never come to mine.

So I would go home.

Alone.

One day Jake stopped me.

He pointed at my bike.

"Look at that old heap!"

He laughed loudly.

"The dumb little girl

has a dumb old heap!"

Some other kids were laughing, too.

"Does that bike even work?"

So I got on my bike.

I was nervous.

But I wanted to show those kids

just how good I was.

I started off on my bike.

I heard a whisper.

"You can do it."

It sounded like Bobby.

Whatever it was,

it made me feel brave.

I did the hardest trick of all.

I spun around and around

without any hands.

Jake's mouth fell open.

"I'd say that bike works, Jake!"

another kid said.

Now kids were laughing—at Jake!

Somehow I had a feeling

he would never bother me again.

I wanted to tell Bobby
what had happened.
Jumping on my bike,
I took off.

I got to the big white house.

But this time Bobby was not out in front.

I left my bike on the porch.

I walked up to the door.

I felt funny about knocking.

After all, Bobby had never asked me

in his house.

A woman came to the door.

She looked down at me.

"Yes? What can I do for you?"

Then she saw my bike.

"Why, look! If it isn't the old bike!"

The lady smiled.

"But how did you know to come here?"

What? What was she talking about?

"I am sorry.

I don't understand," I said.

So the lady went inside.

She came back out with

an old picture.

It was in a fancy silver frame.

The picture was of a bike—my bike.

Only in the picture it looked new.

And next to it, stood a boy.

The boy was wearing

old-fashioned clothes.

It was Bobby!

"My father loved that bike,"

she told me.

And she pointed to the boy in the picture.

"He kept it for years and years.

But after he died,

I gave it away.

I am so glad you are having fun with it."

A strange feeling crept over me.

My heart hammered in my chest,

for suddenly I understood.

"Was your father's name Bobby?"

I asked.

"Why, yes!" the woman said.

"How did you know?"

How could I explain?

Could I say the bike was haunted?

Or that her father was a ghost?

A ghost who helped me

when I needed help.

No. I smiled.

Then I got on my bike and rode away.

I had a feeling my bike

was going to act normal from now on.

I was right.

And I had a feeling

I was not going to see Bobby anymore.

Right again.

In time I made other friends.

But I never forgot Bobby—

my special friend.

And I have never told a soul about him . . .

until now.

DEMCO